TEAM
HERO

D0232844

Special thanks to Michael Ford

*For Lachlan Evans*

ORCHARD BOOKS

First published in Great Britain in 2017 by The Watts Publishing Group

1 3 5 7 9 10 8 6 4 2

Text © 2017 Beast Quest Limited
Cover and inside illustrations by Dynamo
© Beast Quest Limited 2017

Team Hero is a registered trademark in the European Union
Series created by Beast Quest Limited, London

A CIP catalogue record for this book is available from the British Library.

ISBN 978 1 40834 351 7

Printed in Great Britain

The paper and board used in this book are made from wood from responsible sources.
Orchard Books
An imprint of Hachette Children's Group
Part of The Watts Publishing Group Limited
Carmelite House, 50 Victoria Embankment, London EC4Y 0DZ

An Hachette UK Company
www.hachette.co.uk
www.hachettechildrens.co.uk

# TEAM HERO

## BATTLE FOR THE SHADOW SWORD

### ADAM BLADE

ORCHARD

# MEET TEAM HERO ...

## JACK

**POWER:** Super-strength

**LIKES:** Ventura City FC

**DISLIKES:** Bullies

## RUBY

**POWER:** Fire vision

**LIKES:** Comic books

**DISLIKES:** Small spaces

## DANNY

**POWER:** Super-hearing

**LIKES:** Pizza

**DISLIKES:** Thunder

# ... AND THEIR GREATEST ENEMY

# GENERAL GORE

**POWER:** Brilliant warrior

**LIKES:** Carnage

**DISLIKES:** Unfaithful minions

# CONTENTS

# PROLOGUE

CLOUDS OF foul smoke filled
the Great Cavern of Noxx. From
the north wall, a river of lava fell,
crashing into a fiery lake below. On a
high viewing platform carved into a
cliff, Bulk shifted in his leather tunic.
He scratched his warty chin and
watched his master smile cruelly.

"Training is going *perfectly*," said General Gore.

Two warriors circled a giant armoured centipede in a fighting pit below. One was a man with the wings of a huge bat. His hands had deadly sharpened claws, his feet ragged talons. The other fighter was a living skeleton armed with a curved sword.

As the skeleton lunged with his blade, the centipede's tail lashed and coiled around his middle. The crowd around the edges of the pit leaned in, chanting and shaking their fists as the centipede squeezed. But the bat soldier took his chance.

He pounced, claws raised, landing on the centipede's head. The creature writhed, its shriek echoing around the cavern.

Bulk scratched his hairless scalp and shuffled up closer to his master. "General, sir, would it not be better to rest our troops? *Your* troops, I mean?"

General Gore turned, his black cloak whipping round. He fixed Bulk with blazing red eyes that could have melted rock. "Did I ask for your advice?" he snarled.

"N ... n ... no, my lord," said Bulk, quivering.

"You are wise, Master," hissed a voice

from the shadows. "How can you test their mettle properly unless they fight one another?"

Bulk shot a scowl at the other speaker. Smarm seemed almost to slide across the ground, stopping alongside General Gore with his hands clasped in front of him. He wore long robes of brown wool, his gaunt face barely visible under his hood. His hands glowed pale blue with magical energy.

"This time, we will not fail," General Gore declared, driving one gauntleted fist into the palm of his other hand. "Their wretched world will fall at my feet."

Bulk stared out across the vast cavern, where thousands of troops had gathered. Skeletons, bats and centipedes, all armed and ready to rise from Noxx on to the earth's surface — ready for vengeance against the human realm.

"And you can get your sword back, too, my lord," said Smarm, nodding towards the empty scabbard that hung at General Gore's waist.

Their master's face twisted in rage — he didn't like to be reminded of the lost Shadow Sword. Bulk was pleased to see a bead of sweat trickle down Smarm's temple.

"Yes, slave," the General said. "I *will* reclaim what is mine." He raised his arms and bellowed across the cavern. "Enough!"

Silence fell. Every warrior looked up at him.

"I have waited down here in the dark for a thousand years," Gore shouted. "Last time, my forces let me down. But you will *not* repeat that mistake."

Bulk felt his weak heart racing.

"Are you ready for battle?" roared his master.

The army raised their voices in a savage cry, so loud Bulk felt the walls of the cavern tremble. General Gore smiled cruelly, his armour flashing in the orange glow of the lava falls, then strode away from the platform.

Bulk gazed down at the massed troops. *They certainly* look *impressive.*

But a thought wormed into his head. "What about the prophecy?"he muttered.

"Hmm?" said Smarm.

"You know," said Bulk, more loudly.

*"Darkness will rise and conquer light,
unless the Chosen One joins the
fight* ... Doesn't that mean there is
one human up there who can defeat
us?"

A black shape moved quickly out of
the darkness, and Bulk cried out as
a gauntlet gripped him by the throat
and hoisted him off his feet. *General
Gore.* His eyes burning, Gore dangled
Bulk over the edge of the platform.

"Please, my lord," Bulk begged. "I
only meant ..."

Gore's fingers tightened so that
Bulk couldn't breathe. "The prophecy
means nothing," he rasped. "It is a lie

spread by the cowards of Team Hero. No human can defeat me!"

Bulk managed a strangled "Yes, Master," before General Gore tossed

him back on to the platform and
marched off.

# CHAPTER 1

## BEAK THE FREAK

"HEY, BEAK, are you cold or something?" shouted Ricky Evans.

Jack Beacon pretended not to hear. He walked at the back of the group, staring up at the soaring steel skyscrapers of Ventura City. Their windows reflected the bright sun like blazing mirrors.

"Yeah, take your gloves off, freak," called Ricky's friend Olivia.

Jack had heard it all before. He fought the urge to shout something back, remembering what his dad always said — *Just ignore them, Jack.* By the time they got to the City Museum, they'd be bored and the taunts would stop.

His teacher, Mr Parry, stopped to let Jack catch up with him. "Keep up, Jack," he said, rolling his eyes.

"Yes, sir," said Jack.

Besides, he *was* a freak. "Beak the Freak", as the bullies liked to chant. Even the doctors he'd seen couldn't explain what was wrong with his hands.

When they reached the road, the lights changed and Jack and Mr Parry had to wait. The rest of the class were already crossing the square towards the grand columns in front of the City Museum. As Jack watched them, he felt an odd prickle across his neck. Then he noticed someone on the bench opposite. A dark-skinned woman with striking purple hair was gazing right at him.

Jack turned away. He was used to people staring. *She's probably wondering why I'm wearing gloves on such a hot day.*

A bus passed by. When Jack looked again, the woman had vanished.

Jack blinked a couple of times.

"Jack?" said Mr Parry. "We can go now."

The lights had changed. Just as Jack stepped off the pavement, pigeons burst from the square in a cloud of panic and flapping feathers. The ground trembled beneath his feet.

*An earthquake?* Jack wondered, heart thudding. Another tremor shook the earth. Jack heard loud grinding and groaning sounds and struggled to stay upright. A man in a suit tripped and fell. Jack leapt back as the pavement split open in front of him. A crack snaked down across the street, opening wide, so deep he couldn't see the bottom.

People were screaming with panic. A dog on a lead broke from its owner, barking madly. Ricky and Olivia were clutching one another. Jack heard car horns blaring and brakes screeching, the crunch of metal. Then a lorry swerved at speed, slamming into a taxi. Jack's breath caught in his throat as the taxi flipped right over on to its roof and mounted the pavement, spraying white sparks as it slid across the square ...

Straight towards Jack's class.

Without thinking, he threw himself in front of the oncoming car. He clamped his eyes closed and held out his arms. Someone screamed. Half a tonne of metal slammed into him ...

And stopped dead.

Jack opened his eyes.

His gloved hands were buried in the door of the taxi, fingers pressed into the metal. The smell of burned rubber filled his nose. The wheels were still spinning. The driver's door popped open, and a grizzled old man scrambled out, rubbing his head.

"You OK, lad?" he said, gasping.

Jack lifted his hands away, and saw the indented shapes of his fingers in the metal of the door. *What just happened?* He looked around him. His feet hadn't moved an inch.

*I stopped the car like I was catching a ball.*

The earthquake had ended, leaving clouds of dust and a broken pipe spilling water across the street. Car alarms blared. People were crying.

"Did you see that?" cried Olivia. "Beak stopped the car with his hands!"

Jack looked back to see all the

class, and everyone else in the square, staring in his direction. Mr Parry edged towards him, face pale. "Jack, are you hurt?" he asked.

Jack shook his head. He wasn't injured at all. *But that's impossible.* His hands felt hot. He peeled his gloves off, expecting to see the same rough scales he saw every morning before he dressed. "Lizard hands", some kids called them.

But something had changed. His skin was glowing, gold and bright, like it was hooked up to an electric current.

"Whoa," Ricky breathed. "Beak the *Freak!*"

Jack quickly pulled his gloves on again, backing away from the wrecked taxi. It didn't make any sense.

"Jack?" said Mr Parry. "What's going on?"

His teacher was open-mouthed, eyes darting from Jack's hands to his face. He looked afraid.

"I ... don't know," said Jack.

He just wanted to get away. The chant was pounding in his head.

*Beak the Freak. Beak the Freak. Beak the Freak.*

Jack turned and ran, heading down a narrow passage between two shops.

His feet carried him past dustbins and fire doors. He reached a crossroads and ran over without looking, bursting through the gates of the City Park. He raced past the gardens and ponds and play areas until his chest burned. Finally, he sank down against a tree trunk. Around him, the whole city seemed to be spinning. Or maybe it was just his brain.

"That was rather impressive," said a voice next to him.

Startled, Jack scrambled back up. The woman with purple hair was standing beside the tree, a knowing smile on her lips. That didn't make

sense either. He'd just sprinted, as fast as he could, from the City Museum. She had to be fifty years old at least. *No way could she have kept up.*

"How did you get here?" he asked.

Her smile broadened. "That's what I do," she said. "I get to places quickly."

Jack didn't know what to say to that.

"But I'm more interested in what *you* can do." She nodded towards his hands. "That's why I was following you today."

*Following me?* He wondered if she was just a mad lady, but that didn't explain how she'd appeared out of thin air.

"Who are you?" he asked.

The woman held out her hand. "My name is Ms Steel, Jack," she said.

*How does she know my name?*

She didn't *sound* crazy, but he
still wasn't sure he wanted to shake
hands with her.

"I've got to get back to the museum,"
he said. "My teacher will be—"

Ms Steel cocked her head. "Jack,
you won't be going back to school
with Mr Parry."

Jack shivered. She spoke with
complete authority, calm and certain.

"Have you ever felt you didn't
belong?" she asked now, softly. "Like
you were different?" She stared right
into Jack's eyes and he swallowed.

"Always," he mumbled.

"Well, I'm going to take you

somewhere you'll fit right in," said Ms Steel. "Have you heard of Hero Academy?"

## CHAPTER 2

## FIRST DAY AT SCHOOL

JACK AND his parents were the only people on the boat, other than the captain who'd picked them up at Ventura City Port. The city was several miles behind them now, and ahead were the soaring cliffs of Intrepid Island. Shreds of dense fog wreathed its lower reaches, so it seemed to float above the sea on a bed of cloud.

"That nice lady, Ms Steel, said Hero Academy is for students with special talents," said Jack's father. "Maybe all the other kids there have done something brave, just like you did."

Jack knew that his parents were still stunned by what had happened outside the museum three days earlier. So was Jack. None of the authorities believed that a boy had *really* stopped a moving car with just his hands, despite what the witnesses said. But Jack knew something had changed. Inside his gloves, hidden away, his skin still had the same golden glow.

"I'm sure this new school will be just perfect for you," said his mum. "Even if it is hard to find!"

Jack was excited and anxious all at once. He'd never even been away from home before and Hero Academy was a boarding school. He was used to seeing his mum and dad every day. They were the only ones who didn't think he was Beak the Freak — what would it be like not having them around?

The boat's engine dropped a notch as they entered the sea fog. For a few seconds, Jack couldn't see anything in the ghostly cloud, but when they emerged on the other side, looming cliffs rose above them. The captain steered them into a hidden, narrow gorge — it was like travelling into the throat of some huge monster. Jack leaned over the side and watched the dark water slapping against the vessel's hull.

He heard his dad gasp. "Oh, my!"

Jack glanced up. More cliffs circled a vast cove. At the very top stood something like a medieval fortress with stone towers and battlements.

"Is that my *school*?" said Jack, his pulse quickening.

The captain turned and nodded.
"That's Hero Academy."

They crossed the bay to a small jetty. After the captain had moored the boat, Jack and his parents lugged his case over the gangplank. Ms Steel had explained beforehand that this was the point when they'd have to part.

"You have a great time," said his dad, hugging him tight. "I've got a good feeling about this place. I just know they'll accept you for who you are."

"We're so proud of you, Jack," said his mum, kissing his forehead.

Jack watched them get back on board, then waved as the boat pulled away again. He felt very alone.

Jack picked up his case and looked

around. Another boy was standing on the jetty. He looked about Jack's age, with floppy black hair, and he was wearing a silver bodysuit with blue patches on the shoulders.

"I'm Danny," said the stranger. "You're Jack, right? I'll be showing you around the Academy." He grinned, pointing at Jack's Ventura City FC T-shirt. "I support City too! Come on, it's this way."

Jack followed, relief flooding through him. Danny seemed nothing like Ricky or Olivia — he hadn't even mentioned Jack's gloves.

Danny stopped at the bottom of

an enormous flight of steps, where
two stone columns were topped with
statues of eagles.

"It's a long way up!" Jack said,
thinking of his case.

"That's just for show," replied
Danny. He gripped one of the eagle's
wings and tugged. The bottom steps
slid sideways to reveal a gleaming
metal lift.

"Wow!" said Jack, following Danny
inside.

The lift barely seemed to move
but when the doors opened again
they were high up on the windy
battlements. Jack tried to keep the

goofy grin off his lips — they must have travelled hundreds of metres in just a few seconds.

They stepped out on to a walkway overlooking a courtyard, filled with other students all wearing bodysuits in bright colours. Jack struggled to take it all in. Some students were batting a fizzing ball of light back and forth with their hands. Others were zipping between obstacles on sleek motorbikes that floated just above the ground. Another set seemed to be doing some sort of archery practice, wearing visors over their eyes and firing bolts of pure light against

HUMMM...

hovering targets. Jack felt as though he'd stumbled on a sci-fi movie set rather than a school.

"This is *nothing* like my old school," he mumbled. "I'd usually be doing maths right now."

Danny chuckled. "Let's go and get

you a uniform."

He led Jack down a series of stone corridors lined with metal doors, all operated by touch screens. Jack saw signs for things like "Infirmary" and "Refectory", "Archive" and "Research and Development". None of them said

"Science" or "English", or any of the usual school departments.

*Do they even do normal lessons here?* Jack wondered.

"It's a bit of a maze," Danny was saying, as he steered Jack through an automatic glass door, "but you'll get the hang of it."

"How long have you been here?" asked Jack.

"Six weeks," said Danny. "So I'm pretty new too."

"Did someone called Ms Steel ask you to come here?" Jack asked.

"Yeah," said Danny. "When your powers appear, she finds you and tells you about Hero Academy."

"Wow!" The more Jack learned about Hero Academy, the more incredible it became.

They went into one of the rooms. In the centre was a small circular chamber. Its door was open and Jack could see flashing lights inside.

A woman sat at a desk, tapping at a tablet. She looked up and smiled. "Step inside the pod, please," she said, pointing to the chamber. "And you won't need those gloves."

Jack paused. What would Danny and the woman say when they saw what lurked underneath?

"It's OK, Jack," Danny urged him.

Blushing, Jack pulled off the gloves and placed them on the edge of the table. The woman barely batted an eyelid, but Danny's eyes went wide.

"Cool!" he said.

Jack frowned. No one had ever called his condition "cool" before.

"So what's your power?" asked Danny, grinning.

"Power?"

"Yeah, your special ability?" said Danny. "Mine's super-hearing." He pushed back his floppy hair, revealing ears that were three times normal size and pointed like a bat's.

Jack did a double take. Were all the students here different, like him?

"Can you climb walls?" asked Danny. "Trey can do that, too."

Jack remembered the feeling as he'd stopped the taxi — utter control, incredible strength in the lightest of touches. "I ... I don't really know," he said.

Danny smiled crookedly. "I guess we'll find out soon," he said. "Go on — hop in."

Jack walked into the pod uncertainly. "Will it hurt?"

"Oh, no — nothing to worry about!" said the woman. "Hold out your arms and stand still, please. And close your eyes."

Jack did as he was told. He heard a series of thrumming sounds, then sensed a bright flash through his eyelids.

"All done!" said the woman.

Jack looked down and gasped. His jeans and Ventura City FC top had

been replaced with a silver bodysuit like the one Danny was wearing, except Jack's shoulders were red instead of blue. The material was only thin — like a second skin — but he didn't feel in the slightest bit cold.

"You're in Red House," said Danny. "There are four houses at the school — Red, Yellow, Green and Blue. Blue House is the best, obviously!" he added with a grin.

Jack smiled back. "We'll see about that!"

"There are lots of competitions between the houses," Danny explained, "but we have classes

together. We share dormitories, too —
you're in the North Wing dorm with
me. Let's go and dump your stuff
there now."

After more corridors, they reached
the North Wing. This part of Hero
Academy was more like how Jack had
imagined boarding school would be —
long rooms with arched stone ceilings
and narrow windows. The dormitory
Danny led him into was lined with
beds on both sides, with wardrobes,
drawers and desks next to each.

Danny pointed to a bed in the
middle. "That's yours," he said.

As Jack set down his case, he

noticed something in the centre of the
desk and picked it up. It looked like a
wireless earpiece.

"That's your Oracle," Danny explained. He showed Jack his left ear, where a similar device was attached. "Try it."

Jack hooked the Oracle over his ear. "I can't hear anything," he said.

"Of course you can't," said Danny. "You have to talk to it first!"

*What ...?*

"Er, hello?" said Jack.

A voice spoke in his ear. ***"Greetings, Jack. My name is Hawk, and I'm your Oral Response and Combat Learning Escort."***

"Wow," said Jack, glancing at Danny. "What else does it do?"

Before Danny could answer, the earpiece spoke again. *"I can perform a variety of really rather impressive functions, if I say so myself."* Jack grinned at Hawk's words. *"I can provide thermal imaging visors, night sight or X-ray vision. Or GPS and mapping in enemy territory. I'm able to advise on emergency medical procedures to treat battlefield injuries. I also possess comprehensive weapons and tactical knowledge."*

"Wait a minute," said Jack, pulling off the earpiece and looking at Danny. "What's going on? I'm not a soldier!"

Danny's eyebrows shot up. "You are

now!" he said. "Why else do you think you're at Hero Academy?"

JACK STARED at him. "But ..."

A bell echoed from the corridor.

"That's the summons!" said Danny with a grin. "I'll explain later."

Leaving Jack with a hundred different questions, Danny dashed towards the door. Jack hooked the Oracle back over his ear and followed.

They went by a different route this time — round several corners, down a set of steps — and Jack was breathing hard as they emerged at the level of the courtyard. The other students were all lined up, each wearing a silver bodysuit with either red, green, yellow or blue shoulders. A few adults stood around too — one had huge feathered wings folded behind her, and another had diamond-patterned skin, like a snake.

*They're the* teachers? Jack thought, lining up next to Danny. He had to stop himself from staring too hard. What *was* this place?

Everyone was facing a straight-backed, grey-haired man who was wearing a white uniform that buttoned up to his chin. He stood in front of an area cordoned off with a mesh fence. Beyond that barrier, Jack saw a low, circular stone wall. It looked like the outdoor swimming pool at his old school.

"Who's that, Hawk?" he muttered.

*"That, Jack, is Chancellor Rex,"* replied Hawk in his earpiece. *"He's the headmaster here at the Academy."*

"Good morning, heroes," said the Chancellor, "and welcome to Jack Beacon, our newest recruit."

The other students looked at Jack curiously. For a moment he felt uncomfortable, and wished he could hide his scaly hands — then he remembered he didn't have to.

"I called you together because I have grave news," said the Chancellor. He nodded, and two of the older pupils began to move the mesh fence aside. "I want you all to come closer," he said.

With low mutterings, the students edged forward. Jack gasped as he saw what lay within the wall. It wasn't a pool at all but a pit. At its base were horribly life-like statues, moss-covered and flaking. There were skeletons wielding swords — one with its jaws open in a silent scream, another missing an arm — and things like giant bats, wings spread as if about to fly away.

*Why would anyone carve something so terrifying?* Jack thought.

"As most of you know," said Chancellor Rex, "Hero Academy was founded one thousand years ago after Team Hero defeated the army of warriors from the realm of Noxx. This portal was their gateway to the earth's surface."

Jack wondered if this was some

sort of weird joke. He cast a glance
at Danny, but for once the other boy
wasn't smiling.

"Brave heroes fought to save
humanity from these creatures,"
continued the Chancellor. "They were

successful, but many lost their lives."

"Those things were *real*?" whispered
Jack.

At his side, Danny nodded, then
his eyes travelled past Jack. Jack
turned and saw, high up on one of the

courtyard walls, a lizard-like creature, with a misshapen human head and scaly armour. His clawed hands held a spiked mace on a chain.

"That one was called Raptrix," Danny murmured. "He killed many of our warriors in the last invasion."

Jack shuddered. *Surely I'm dreaming this ...*

"The first heroes closed this portal," said Chancellor Rex, "and built Hero Academy here to guard it. Over the centuries the heroes of the Academy have fought many enemies. But we always knew our oldest foe would one day strike again." He paused. "That moment has arrived."

A buzz of shocked surprise broke throughout the ranks of students.

"Our research tells us that the recent earthquakes in Ventura City were unnatural," said the Chancellor. "We believe the Noxxians are stirring."

He held out both hands and reached upwards. Jack saw the Chancellor's eyelids flutter as a strange breeze whipped across the courtyard. Then an image appeared in the air above them — blurred at first, but becoming clearer. Jack looked on, his throat going dry.

It was a man, clad completely in black armour, with a black cloak swirling around him. And beyond him were rows and rows of soldiers, the glint of weapons, the distant echoes of angry cries.

"How on earth are we seeing that?" asked Jack.

"That's his power," said Danny. "Chancellor Rex can show the future. Some of it, anyway."

"Students trained here at Hero Academy have protected this world for generations," said Chancellor Rex, "but you will soon face your greatest ever test. We thought General Gore

was dead, but we were wrong. He is
alive — and he is returning."

The heavily armoured man seemed
to stare right at Jack with eyes like
red-hot coals.

The image faded, but Jack thought he could still feel the heat from the general's burning gaze.

"Be ready to fight, all of you," said the Chancellor. "We have alerted our bases around the world, but the attack could come at any moment. Be on your guard. We are humanity's only defence against Noxx."

The students broke rank, muttering grimly with one another. Jack's heart thumped in his chest. He didn't feel like a guardian of *anything*, but if he could help stand up to these forces of Noxx, he would.

"It's a lot to take in, I know." The

voice belonged to Ms Steel, appearing beside Jack out of nowhere.

Startled, Jack stepped back and collided with a girl about his age, who had yellow shoulders on her bodysuit.

"Hey, watch it!" she said.

"Sorry," said Jack, taking in her dark curly hair and scowling features.

The girl's face softened to a mischievous grin. "You'll get used to Ms Steel and her teleporting."

Jack managed to smile back. "This place is getting weirder by the second."

"Jack, meet Ruby," said Ms Steel. "She's only been here for a week." She beckoned Danny over too, and as she did so the ring she wore on her index finger flashed in the sun. Its jewel was shaped like a cat's eye. "You three are our newest students," Ms Steel went on. "And it looks like I found you all just in time."

Jack noticed that Ruby had the strangest eyes he'd ever seen — they were almost orange.

"I'd suggest you all get to know each

other," said Ms Steel. "Lessons start in a few minutes. Why don't you show each other your skills before then?"

Jack looked across at Danny, who was pushing his hair back to expose his bat ears.

"Let's do it," said Ruby, rubbing her hands together.

Jack hadn't tried to use his super-strength since the day of the earthquake — he'd been anxious, scared even about what might happen. "I'm not sure I—" he began to say.

But Ms Steel had vanished.

"Like I said, you'll get used to her,"

said Ruby. "So, let's see what you can both do."

Danny pointed to a pair of students with red panels on the shoulders of their suits, who were walking across the battlements far above.

"The guy on the left is saying he's looking forward to sending General Gore right back where he came from," Danny said. "And the one on the right ... well, he's saying it's probably all a false alarm."

Jack stared at him. "You can really hear that from here?"

Danny narrowed his eyes. "I can also hear someone laying the tables in the refectory through three feet of stone," he said proudly, "and the waves crashing on the cliff-face down at the shore."

Jack stared at him in amazement. "Have you always been able to do that?" he asked.

Danny flicked the tip of one of his ears. "I was born with these," he said. "I only got super-hearing about a month ago, though. There was a massive fire in the block of flats where I live. I could hear that an old lady who lived on the top floor was trapped, so I ran back into the building to help her." He shook back his floppy hair. "When I got her outside, Ms Steel appeared and told me about Hero Academy. She'd sensed that I'd come into my power."

"Wow," said Jack. "How about you, Ruby?"

"Check this out." Ruby put her fingertips to both her temples and stared at the mesh fence. A stream of flame shot from her eyes, and a moment later smoke rose, as the metal began to glow red-hot. Danny clapped.

"That's incredible!" said Jack.

Ruby shut off the ray, and pushed a curl off her face. "Thanks," she said. "I

used to hate my orange eyes, but one day my parents and my little sister and I were all in the car, on our way to visit my grandma. While we were going over a bridge, there was an accident. A lorry drove into us. Our car went right off the bridge and fell into the river."

"That must have been terrifying," Jack said.

Ruby nodded. "It was. The car was sinking and we couldn't get out. But somehow I just knew that if I focused really hard on one of the doors, I could save us. I didn't expect to burn the door open, though! We swam out

and made it to the shore. Then guess
what?"

Jack grinned. "Ms Steel appeared?"

"Exactly," said Ruby. "So what
about you, Jack? What's your power?"

Jack showed her his scaly hands.
"These, I guess. I stopped a moving
car with them."

"Wow — that's some serious
strength," said Danny. He pointed
towards a hoverbike parked up across
the courtyard. "Do you think you
could lift that?"

"I can try," said Jack. He took a
few steps towards the bike, suddenly
doubting himself. But as he raised his

hands, he saw them glowing just like they had done back by the museum. It was almost as if he could feel his heart pumping extra blood through his arms. He slipped one hand under the handlebars and another under the saddle. With barely any effort at all, he lifted the bike over his head.

"That's awesome!" Ruby cried.

But Danny wasn't smiling. His face was pale. "I can hear something." He swallowed. "It's coming from underground."

Then Jack felt it too, through the soles of his feet — a tremor, then a rumble. Within the low stone wall,

the statues began to tremble. Jack
set the bike down quickly.

"What's going on?" asked Ruby.
"Did we do something?"

A crack widened in the centre of
the ancient portal, as great chunks
of earth fell away.

"We should find Chancellor Rex,"
said Jack. "This doesn't look ..."

His voice dried up in his throat
as something thrust out from the
ground — a huge head, much larger
than Jack himself, that writhed
on a segmented, armoured body.
Bristling pincers trailed slime over
a gaping mouth, lined with teeth.

The creature spilled out over the crumbling ground, and with it came shreds of thick shadow.

Jack tried to make sense of what he was seeing — a giant centipede, eyes burning a fierce and sickly yellow. He knew only one thing for certain.

The Noxx invasion had just begun.

# CHAPTER 4

## ZARNIK

THE REST of the centipede warrior came trailing over the edge of the stone wall. To his horror, Jack saw that each segment had hairy arms, and each arm clutched something like a crossbow. But the arrows that shimmered on their strings looked like they were made of pure light, fizzing with energy.

Jack's heart thumped hard enough to burst from his chest. His hands were glowing brighter than ever, as if the adrenaline in his blood was supercharging them. "What is that thing, Hawk?" he said.

*"Meet Zarnik,"* said Hawk. *"He's one of General Gore's nastier lieutenants. Height: 2 metres. Length: 16 metres. Weight—"*

"It's OK," Jack interrupted. "You can tell me later."

He wasn't sure what to do, but he stood his ground. The creature turned his huge head towards Jack and his pincers clacked wetly.

"Find the Shadow Sword," Zarnik growled, "or face the wrath of our master."

"Who's he talking to?" said Ruby, pressing closer to Danny protectively.

"And what's the Shadow Sword?" Jack wondered aloud.

Behind Zarnik, smaller centipedes appeared from the portal, each the size of the hoverbike Jack had lifted a few moments ago. They were almost identical to the larger creature. Beady yellow eyes goggled as they scurried on furry legs, swarming across the courtyard towards the school buildings, crossbows on their backs.

Danny ran to the edge of the courtyard and pulled on a rope. The summons bell rang out again. Seconds later, students and teachers came dashing back out of the school building.

"Jack, look out!" shouted Ruby.

He turned and saw one of the centipede creatures darting towards him. Jack cried out, raising his hands, and felt it collide into him. He thrust out his palms and the creature went flying through the air. As it splatted into the wall, it exploded into shadows.

"Nice work!" said Danny.

Jack looked at his hands in amazement. *Did I do that?*

Something ploughed into his back and he hit the ground face-first. Rolling over, he saw another of the creatures rearing up over him, its claws raised.

"Die, human!" it screeched.

Then an orange beam of fire flashed into its body. The creature melted into black smoke.

"Thank me later!" said Ruby.

Jack picked himself up. Black shadows were snaking from the portal like the tentacles of a monstrous squid, searching for prey. Chancellor Rex was up on the battlements of the school, waving his arms.

"Don't let the shadow touch you!" he cried. "It will turn you into a slave of Noxx!"

Jack's heart almost stopped as he saw one of the mini centipedes scrambling over the stone battlement of the fortress, heading right for the Chancellor.

"Look out!" Jack shouted.

Just as the centipede was about to reach the top, Ruby fried it with her fire beam. Jack tugged her back as a whip of shadow lashed out towards them.

The other students and teachers were also doing battle with the minions of Zarnik. Energy bolts zapped across the courtyard from blasters clutched by a band of older students from Green House. One of the creatures rose into the air and

Jack saw a girl in a Red House suit on the ground, controlling it remotely with her hands. With a flinging motion, she hurled it back through the portal.

One of the teachers was spinning so fast, he was like a tornado as he charged between the centipedes, sending them flying in all directions.

"Help!" cried Danny.

Jack spotted his friend surrounded by three creatures. Two of the minions snapped at Danny's legs, dragging him down. Jack began to run, but he knew he wouldn't make it in time. Danny cried out as the third centipede aimed at his head with its pincers.

*No!* Jack thought.

Then the air shimmered, revealing Ms Steel. She swung her staff at the first two centipedes, smashing them

aside. The other looked up in shock. Jack ran right into it, grabbing it around the middle. Its legs scrabbled, and it screeched in fury, but Jack's desperation drove him on. He spun round twice, then threw the creature with all his strength, sending it crashing into a wall.

"Thanks!" said Danny, scrambling up.

There were still a dozen or so centipedes doing battle around the portal. Ms Steel vanished and reappeared in the blink of an eye, thrusting and spinning her staff among the fighting. One student, dressed in a Red House suit, was blowing blue air from her lips, freezing the foes in place like ice statues. Another, from Yellow House, was taking huge leaps like a human flea, crashing down on them from above.

But Jack's heart sank as he realised that some students were injured and being hurried back into the school by their friends, their clothes ripped by scorch marks from their enemies' crossbows.

"Defend the battlements!" the teacher with skin like a snake was instructing the other students. "They cannot be allowed to enter the school!"

Jack leapt back as a lick of shadow from the portal lashed towards him. Zarnik, the centipedes' leader, had vanished.

*Has he run away?*

"What do they want?" shouted Ruby.

"The big one said something about a sword!" said Danny.

"The Shadow Sword," Jack said, remembering. "Hawk?"

*"I'm delighted that you asked,"* said Hawk. *"The Shadow Sword is an ancient weapon that once belonged to General Gore. During the last great conflict, General Gore lost it in battle.*

*It is rumoured to be locked in a secret chamber beneath Hero Academy, though no human has the power to wield it."*

Danny cocked his head. "I can hear something underground again. Footsteps. Lots of them."

"From the portal?" asked Jack in despair. He didn't know if they'd be able to handle any more Noxxians.

Danny shook his head. "No." He pointed towards the school buildings. "I think it's coming from over there."

Jack looked and saw a mound of loose earth and stone at the edge of the courtyard. A trail of slime led to a dark hole in the ground. He rushed over with Ruby and Danny, and found himself staring into a roughly hewn tunnel burrowing beneath the wall. "That must be where Zarnik's gone," he said. "Should we find Chancellor Rex?"

Ruby shook her head. "No time! We have to stop Zarnik!" She ran into the tunnel.

Jack glanced back at the fight. He couldn't tell if they were winning. And Ruby was right, if they went to get help, it could be too late.

*It's up to us to stop Zarnik finding the Shadow Sword.*

"Let's go!" he said, plunging into the darkness with Danny at his side.

# CHAPTER 5

## THE SHADOW SWORD

THE ONLY light in the tunnel came from the glow of Jack's hands. The air was musty and cold, the tunnel walls crumbling. At times they had to duck, or even crawl on all fours. More of the sticky slime hung in patches from the ceiling, and Jack stayed well clear. Clumps of earth and small rocks fell from the roof.

*I hope it doesn't cave in*, he thought.

He guessed they were about twenty metres below the courtyard when the tunnel burst out into an underground corridor. This one was man-made, with

stone arches supporting the roof. It looked like something you'd find in a medieval cathedral, and must have been hundreds of years old. Simple weapons lined the walls — swords and spears, pikes and shields and maces.

"I can hear breathing," muttered

Danny, plucking a spear down from the wall.

Jack picked up a double-headed axe. He'd expected it to be heavy, but his scaly hands wielded it easily.

"Aren't you going to take a weapon?" Jack asked Ruby.

She tapped her temples and her eyes flared orange for a moment. "I've got what I need already."

They edged along the gloomy corridor. Strands of spider-webs hung from the ceiling, broken apart already by Zarnik.

*He must be crawling on the ceiling,* thought Jack, with a squirm in his gut.

A door at the end lay in splintered ruins. Jack paused on the threshold and strained to look into the dark beyond. Fear ran its fingers down his spine.

"How are we even supposed to see without a torch?" he mumbled, holding up the axe.

*"May I suggest night-vision settings?"* Hawk said, into Jack's ear.

"Er ... yes," said Jack. "Thanks, Hawk."

He heard a tiny whir, and then a plasma visor extended from the Oracle over his eyes. The world flickered into shades of green.

"Wow! I can see everything!"

"Cool, huh?" said Danny.

Jack looked round to see both of his friends had visors over their eyes, too. There were slits in Ruby's so she could fire her beams through it.

"Let's go," said Ruby.

Jack nodded and stepped into a vast chamber. It was perhaps only five metres from floor to ceiling, but it stretched for many more in every other direction. Squat pillars held up the roof, and the walls were bare, black brick, crumbling in places. It made Jack think of a burial chamber beneath a church.

Danny tugged his arm. "There!" he whispered, pointing.

A huge shadow flickered across one of the pillars.

*Zarnik.*

The shadow vanished.

They crept along from one pillar

to the next. Even Jack's normal ears could hear the rattle of the centipede's clawed feet on the stone-flagged floor. But where was he?

Jack stopped. The air felt suddenly colder, or perhaps it was just fear chilling the blood in his veins. His eyes flicked sideways and fell on something he couldn't make sense of at first. It was the hilt of a sword, black and smoky. The blade itself was buried in the floor.

"The Shadow Sword," he breathed. Ruby and Danny came to his side.

"Correct," rasped a voice from above. Jack looked up to see Zarnik clinging to the ceiling. His hideous body peeled from the stone, segment by segment. Several of Zarnik's crossbows were trained on Jack and his friends.

"Run!" Jack cried, shoving Danny as the energy arrows rained down. Sparks flew around them as they wove in and out of the columns. Jack lost sight of his friends and the sword, pressing his back up against a pillar with his axe clutched close to his body.

"Is everyone OK?" Danny called, his voice echoing.

"I am!" said Ruby.

"Me too!" said Jack. His hands were

sweating on the handle of the axe.
He peered out and saw Zarnik edging
along one of the aisles, eyes swivelling.

*If I can distract him, maybe one of
the others will be able to sneak up
and take him down.*

He stepped out, brandishing the axe.

"Brave boy," hissed the giant
centipede, antennae bristling. "Brave
but foolish."

The centipede surged forward,
jaws dripping with strings of sticky
membrane. But in the same instant
Danny charged from one side, driving
his spear into the creature's side

Zarnik lashed out with his tail.

The tip struck Danny in the middle
and hurled him into a column. He
crumpled up with a groan.

"No!" Jack roared. He swung his axe,

but the blade bounced harmlessly off Zarnik's armoured head. Jack slashed again, with all his strength. The axe slid off and buried itself with a *thwack* in one of the stone columns.

"Pathetic," rasped Zarnik.

"Try this!" shouted Ruby. The whole chamber was suddenly bright with the orange blaze of her fire beams. They struck Zarnik's head and the centipede curled up with a shriek. Ruby pressed forward, fingers to her temples, keeping the beams focused on their foe. After a few seconds, she collapsed with a gasp. "I can't keep it up for long," she said.

"We've got company!" mumbled Danny, staggering to his feet.

Jack saw that Zarnik's minions were coming through the shattered door with cautious, scuttling movements. He tried to free the axe-head, but it was jammed in the stone.

"Take care of the humans," growled Zarnik to the centipede creatures. He unfurled his body and sped deeper into the chamber ...

Towards the Shadow Sword.

Danny lunged at one of the minions with his spear. It melted into black swirls. Another scrabbled towards Ruby, only to be blasted to shadows by her fire beam. But more were coming.

"Jack, go after Zarnik!" panted Danny. "Ruby and I will hold the others off."

Jack didn't hesitate. Leaving the axe, he plunged through the chamber after the giant centipede.

He made it only a few steps before one of Zarnik's minions fired a shaft of energy, which sizzled past his face. He ducked beneath another. Then something snagged his ankle and he hit the ground. One of the centipedes coiled around his middle, squeezing hard. Jack drove his fingers into the creature's flesh and swung it through the air into a pillar. With a squeal, it vanished into black shadows.

Jack snatched up the crossbow it had left behind then staggered on. He heard the clash and fizz of the others still battling.

His heart lifted as he found the sword still buried in the

ground. But Zarnik's shape also slid into view, eyes glittering. Jack planted his feet between the giant centipede and its prize, levelling the crossbow.

"You don't give up, do you?" said Zarnik, pincers clicking.

With a hiss, the creature of Noxx spat a mouthful of slime that hit Jack right in the face. He tripped backwards, dropping the crossbow, clawing at his visor. When at last it was clear, he saw Zarnik rearing over him, ready to crash down.

Desperately, Jack scrabbled for a weapon. His fingers closed on something terribly cold. As Zarnik's body fell towards him, jaws bared, he threw up his hands.

It was over.

# CHAPTER 6

## THE CHOSEN ONE

ZARNIK'S BODY came to a shuddering halt on top of Jack. The centipede's pincers opened and closed, inches from his face. The antennae trembled. Jack realised he was holding the hilt of a black sword, and that the blade was buried deep in Zarnik's chest.

*The Shadow Sword!*

With a terrible roar, the monster dissolved into smoky black shadows and the weight pressing down on Jack was gone.

"What happened to the creatures?" came Danny's voice, echoing further off in the chamber.

"They just vanished!" answered Ruby. "Where's Jack?"

"I ... I'm here," Jack managed to say, peeling himself off the floor. He still clutched the sword — it throbbed slightly in his grip, like a living thing.

Ruby and Danny came rushing between the pillars. Both their

uniforms were torn and scorched, and
Ruby's cheek was bleeding from a cut.
As they saw him, their feet slowed.

"Whoa!" said Danny. "That's the
Shadow Sword! How did you ...?"

"I don't know," said Jack, swishing
the blade slowly back and forth.
Though it seemed to weigh almost
nothing, he sensed the power in the
ancient blade ... and its evil core.

"Where's Zarnik?" asked Ruby.

"I ... the sword — it killed him," said
Jack.

Danny's eyes lit up. "Wow!" he said.
"I guess that's why all the critters
disappeared as well." He patted Jack

on the back. "You saved the whole school!"

Jack blushed. "I was lucky," he said. "The sword was just there. Anyway, it was you guys doing all the real fighting."

"Let's go and find the Chancellor," said Ruby, grinning. She nodded to the sword. "I think he'll want to see that too."

Jack smiled back. *What a crazy first day at school!*

● ● ●

In the courtyard, the other students and teachers were standing in tired clusters, or tending to those lying on the ground. Jack looked on anxiously.

"Take the injured to the infirmary,"
Chancellor Rex was calling.

"And if it's full, use the school
hall," added Ms Steel, surveying the
devastation.

Her gaze came to rest on Jack and
her lips parted in astonishment. She
nudged the headmaster. His eyes
went wide as he took in the Shadow
Sword.

"That's *impossible!*" he gasped.

Black shadows still swirled in the
portal, but there was no sign of any
more of the enemy. One by one, the
other students all turned to look at

Jack and his companions.

"Jack got rid of Zarnik!" said Ruby proudly.

Jack saw disbelieving faces, heads shaking. No one seemed to want to come close. It was just like the day by the museum — the frightened stares and confusion.

Chancellor Rex leant close to Ms Steel and whispered something to her. Her mouth gaped.

Jack felt himself blush again. *They're talking about me.*

"What's the 'Chosen One'?" asked Danny.

Ms Steel smiled. "I forgot about

Danny's power," she said. "No point whispering, Chancellor."

Chancellor Rex raised an eyebrow. "There was once a prophecy," he said, staring at Jack so intently that he had to look away. "*Darkness will rise and conquer light, unless the Chosen One joins the fight.*"

"What does that have to do with me?" asked Jack.

"Many great warriors have tried to pull the Shadow Sword from the ground," said the Chancellor, "but all have failed. Until today."

"It can't be a coincidence that you've come into your powers now," said Ms Steel solemnly. "If you can wield that sword, then you must be immune to shadow. Hero Academy needs you, Jack. You must be the one the prophecy speaks of."

Jack didn't know what to say. He didn't even know his way around the school yet. He'd had no training. He wasn't a hero — he was just a boy from Ventura City.

Ms Steel came to his side. "I sense your doubts," she said. "But if the Chancellor is right, destiny lies in your grasp." She pointed towards the portal. "It is said that the Shadow Sword has the power to open and close the pathways to Noxx. Use it now — thrust it into the shadows and close the portal once more."

The students parted as Jack walked uncertainly towards the low stone wall, with Danny and Ruby at his side. His whole body ached from the fighting. The portal spat and bubbled like a pit of black lava. Ms Steel said he was immune to shadow, but even so, Jack was careful. He didn't want to risk becoming one of General Gore's soldiers — a creature of the darkness. But as he held the sword aloft, the shadows retreated, as if driven by a fierce wind.

Jack paused, full of doubt. Looking back over his shoulder, he saw the expectant faces watching. Danny nodded.

Turning the blade point-down

in his glowing hands, Jack drove
it into the shadows, up to the hilt.
The black swirls danced and lashed,
flickering like oil thrown onto flames.
Several students jumped back, and
one licking shadow came so close to
Danny that he tripped backwards
and landed on his behind. Jack felt
the power surging through the sword,
making it tremble in his hand. Then,
like a sea freezing to ice, the shadow
began to harden, transforming into
dull grey stone.

Jack realised silence had fallen over
the courtyard. He almost expected to
hear the chant. *Beak the Freak. Beak*

*the Freak.*

Instead, the students began to clap. Jack felt a slow smile creeping over his lips as the cheers rose to a roar of triumph.

*I did it!*

As the applause died, Chancellor Rex held up his hands. His face alone still looked serious.

"Students of Hero Academy, we have won the first battle," he said. "But we still face a deadly conflict. A war has started today. General Gore will open more portals. Zarnik was one foe among thousands, and there will be others far more dangerous."

Jack's eyes scanned the faces of his fellow students. They were all kids, the oldest maybe sixteen. But they looked determined.

*If we stick together, we have a chance*, he thought.

"For now, enjoy your victory," said the Chancellor. "There will be a feast in the refectory."

The students began to file out towards the main buildings, many stopping to congratulate Jack.

"You're a hero!" said Danny, dusting down his bodysuit.

"I don't know about that!" said another boy as he walked past. His bodysuit had green patches and his jet black hair was cut short. "Like the Chancellor said, Zarnik wasn't that big a deal."

Ruby scowled. "Oh really, Olly? I'd like to have seen you take him on."

"Don't worry," Olly said. "You'll soon see what I can do." He stalked off, joining a group of other Green House students.

"Ignore him," said Danny.

Jack smiled and nodded. *Olly's*

*right, though*, he thought. *I only just managed to defeat Zarnik. How many more fights can we win?*

"Hey, that shadow almost got you!" he said to Danny, trying to change the subject.

A fleeting frown crossed Danny's features, then passed. "Yeah, but it didn't," he said quickly.

Ruby gave him a playful punch on the arm. "Good, because it sounds like we're going to have enough enemies to fight already! We don't need you turning into a Noxxian too. I'd have to fry you with my death stare."

Danny laughed. "Just try it!"

Jack and his friends trailed after the other students heading towards the dining hall.

"Come on," said Danny. "The food here is *great*, but it's first come first served. Don't want the green-suits getting all the good stuff."

Jack followed the others inside. In just one day, his whole life had changed. He had friends. He belonged. Already he felt part of something bigger, just as Ms Steel had promised. But the *Chosen One*? The one who would defeat General Gore's armies? It seemed impossible.

One thing was certain, though. He

wasn't Beak the Freak any longer. He was Jack Beacon of Hero Academy, the last defence against evil.

And with his new friends at his side, he would face it with all his might.

READ ON TO LEARN
MORE ABOUT WHY
# HERO ACADEMY
WAS CREATED...

# TIMETABLE

|  | MON | TUE | WED | THUR | FRI |
|---|---|---|---|---|---|
| 08.00 | ASSEMBLY | ASSEMBLY | ASSEMBLY | ASSEMBLY | ASSEMBLY |
| 09.00 | POWERS | POWERS | POWERS | POWERS | POWERS |
| 10.00 | COMBAT | STRATEGY | TECH | COMBAT | STRATEGY |
| 11.00 | MATHS | GEOGRAPHY | ENGLISH | HISTORY | ENGLISH |
| 12.00 | HISTORY | SCIENCE | MATHS | SCIENCE | GEOGRAPHY |
| 13.00 | | | LUNCH! | | |
| 14.00 | TECH | COMBAT | COMBAT | STRATEGY | WEAPON TRAINING |
| 15.00 | GYM | GYM | WEAPON TRAINING | GYM | GYM |
| 16.00 | GYM | GYM | GYM | GYM | HOMEWORK |
| 17.00 | HOMEWORK | HOMEWORK | HOMEWORK | HOMEWORK | FREE |

and many from oth...
had special powers, and knew each...
once a year at a secret tournament to practise their...
skills. Each of these warriors raised their own army of
...iers to do battle against the Noxxians. But Gretchen
...were strong enough to win. She wanted
...fight alongside them, and she

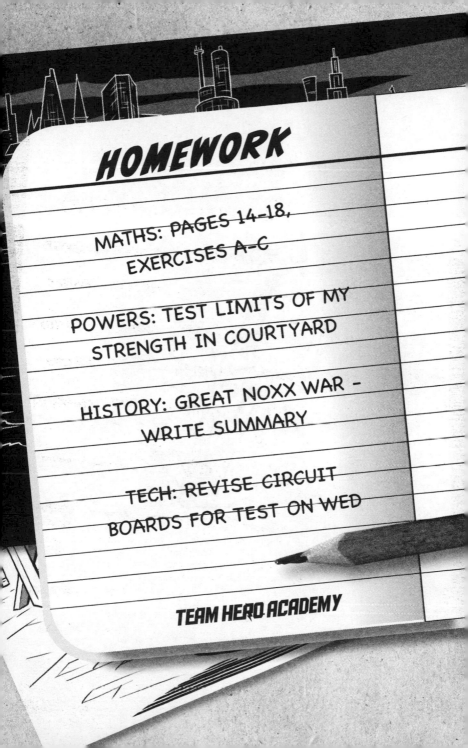

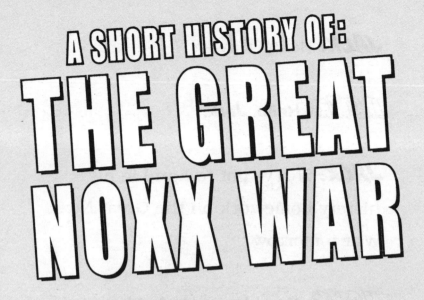

# A SHORT HISTORY OF: THE GREAT NOXX WAR

**DAY:** *TUESDAY*

**TIME:** *6.32PM, JUST AFTER DINNER*

**LOCATION:** *HERO ACADEMY LIBRARY*

**JACK:** Hello? Hawk?

**HAWK:** Hello, Jack.

**JACK:** So, I've got to hand in my history homework on the Great Noxx War tomorrow.

**HAWK:** Yes, I know, Jack. I have access to your timetable, your homework assignments and your marks. Maths isn't your best subject, is it?

**JACK:** Uh, well, it's not my favourite, I guess. But back to the Great Noxx

War ... Can you help me? Professor Soren wants us all to write five pages and I hardly know anything about it. When did the war begin?

**HAWK:** *I'd be delighted to help. Scanning for data ... Here it is. So, the Great Noxx War began one thousand years ago, when the world was very different. There was no Ventura City, no Hero Academy, and definitely no Oracles.*

**JACK:** Homework back then must have been a nightmare.

**HAWK:** That was the least of everyone's problems ... The portal that's now in the school courtyard opened, and General Gore led an army out of Noxx to conquer the surface of the earth. That was the start of the war, but the invasion had been planned long before this – and not by Gore.

**JACK:** Wait, I thought Gore was in charge?

**HAWK:** He is indeed in charge of Noxx. But Noxx isn't the only realm in the centre of the earth – there are many others. The rulers of these

**realms sit on a council called the High Command. And the head of the council is the Supreme Master.**

*JACK:* So the Supreme Master is General Gore's boss?

*HAWK8* **Exactly. The Supreme Master created the shadow you saw spilling out of the portal. As you know, it's a terrible weapon that turns all it touches to evil. The Supreme Master needed a warrior strong enough to spread this shadow over the surface of the earth. And in Gore, he found the perfect man for the job. He made**

*Gore a general and put him in charge of Noxx.*

**JACK:** What was Gore doing before then?

**HAWK:** Well, Team Hero historians aren't sure. Some think he rose up through the ranks of the Noxxian soldiers. Some think he isn't from Noxx at all, and came from one of the other realms ruled by the High Command. Maybe we'll never know the truth ... All the historians agree on one thing, though: General Gore was the most brilliant warrior the High Command had ever had. Gore started preparing for battle. The Noxxians couldn't bear daylight, so when the night was at its darkest, he launched his invasion.

**JACK:** Who tried to stop him?

**HAWK:** No one at first, I'm sorry to say. The invasion was a horrible shock and Gore's soldiers were terrifying – skeletons armed with swords, bat creatures and centipede monsters. Many people just fled in fear. At first the Noxxians fought only at night, and spent the daylight hours hiding underground. But their evil presence gradually spread a veil of darkness over the sky. Soon there was no difference between night and day, and the Noxxians could attack constantly. They achieved many victories. But a band of heroes was preparing to fight back.

**JACK:** Hero Force!

**HAWK:** They weren't called Hero Force yet, but they soon would be. The heroes were led by Gretchen of Ventura, a young warrior armed with a bow and arrow and the power of super-speed. Ventura was a village then, on the site where Ventura City stands today. Gretchen gathered a group of warriors to take on General Gore and his forces. One warrior was from the desert realm of Solus, another from the underwater realm of Sequana, and many from other lands around the world. The warriors had special powers, and knew each other well – for generations they had been meeting once a year at a secret tournament to practise their fighting skills. Each of these warriors raised their own army of soldiers to do battle against the Noxxians. But Gretchen wasn't sure they were strong enough to win. She wanted the greatest warrior of all to fight alongside them, and she searched everywhere for him — but he was nowhere to be found.

**JACK:** Who was he?

**HAWK:** His name was Wulfstan Hightower. He had super-strength, just like you, and was skilled with any weapon. But a few years before the Noxx invasion, Wulfstan went missing. Gretchen and her allies didn't know if they could win without him.

**JACK:** But they did, right?

*HAWK:* **Yes, after a hard battle. Without Wulfstan the fighting was very difficult, but they managed it. The warriors' armies worked closely together, and their teamwork helped drive the Noxxians back. But what decided the battle was the moment Gretchen discovered the Orb of Lux.**

*JACK:* What was that? A weapon?

*HAWK:* **By my calculations, the most powerful weapon ever created. The orb was a glowing ball of magical light. A knight from the Order of Lux, a secret organisation sworn to protect the orb,** led Gretchen to it. She ran with the orb at super-speed, then released it up into the sky. It struck the veil of darkness and shattered it. Daylight broke through – and the armies of Noxx were turned to ash.

**JACK:** Wow! So the Noxxians don't like light? I wonder how Zarnik was able to attack in the daytime ... Did Gretchen and the others set up Team Hero after they'd won?

**HAWK:** That's right. It was a global organisation of fighters with special powers, sworn to defend humanity –

*just as it is today. They also built Hero Academy here on Intrepid Island, to train young heroes how to use their powers so they could join the ranks of the force. But despite all this success, Gretchen never stopped wondering about Wulfstan Hightower. She still held out hope that he would return one day. He never did.*

**JACK:** Unlike General Gore ... We'll have to make sure we beat him again, like the first heroes did. Thanks, Hawk, this is brilliant — I've got loads to write about now.

*HAWK:* My pleasure, Jack. Now, shall I download some extra maths tuition for you? I've got some fascinating algebra problems I think you'll enjoy.

*JACK:* Er, maybe another time ...

READ ON FOR A SNEAK
PEEK AT BOOK 2:

ATTACK OF THE BAT ARMY

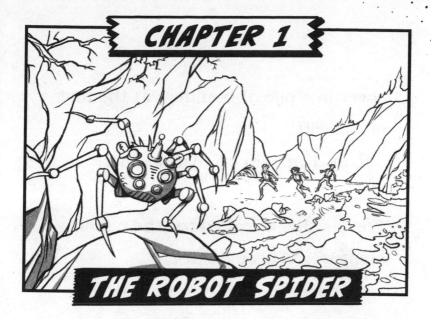

# CHAPTER 1

## THE ROBOT SPIDER

JACK BEACON raced across the
beach towards the towering cliff-
face. Gulls screeched overhead and
the surf crashed against the rocky
shoreline. Beside him ran his friends,
Danny and Ruby. Jack saw the
robotic spider they were chasing
skitter over the shingle. It dived for

cover in a pile of boulders at the foot of the cliff.

Ruby leapt up on to a boulder, shaking her curly black hair from her eyes as she searched for the metal creature. "Where did it go?"

"Careful," Danny puffed. "Those rocks look slippery."

Ruby ignored him. "There!" she cried.

Jack watched, impressed, as Ruby sprang lightly from boulder to boulder. She wasn't scared of anything.

"Looks like we'd better follow her," said Jack.

Danny groaned. "Can't we have a rest first?"

"We've got to be back at school by lunchtime, remember?" said Jack. "So we've only got twenty minutes left to catch the spider."

Danny rubbed his eyes and Jack noticed how tired his friend looked.

"Are you OK?" Jack asked.

"I didn't sleep well," said Danny. "You probably kept the whole dormitory awake with your snoring."

Jack gave him a friendly shove. "It's not my fault you've got super-hearing! Anyway, I don't snore."

"How do you know?" Danny said, but he was grinning. "I'm definitely wearing earplugs tonight."

They clambered over the pile of rocks until they caught up with Ruby. She was crouched next to a huge boulder.

"The spider's crawled under there," she said. "I can't get it out."

Danny nudged Jack. "I bet you can!"

Jack took a firm grip of the boulder with his scaly, golden hands. His super-strength tingled through him like an electric current as he lifted the enormous rock over his head.

Before Jack had started at Hero Academy, just two weeks ago, he'd always worn gloves to stop people seeing his hands. But now he was proud of them. Everyone at Hero

Academy was
different, all
with some kind
of special power.

Carefully, he
placed the boulder
to one side.

"Thanks, Jack!"
Ruby said. "Look!"

The spider was half buried in sand,
crouched low on its spiky metal legs.
Ruby reached to grab it — but it
scuttled away with lightning speed,
heading for the cliff-face.

"Come on!" Jack shouted.

They dashed after it. The spider

stopped at the base of the cliff. It twitched its tiny antennae.

Jack drew the Shadow Sword from his belt. It felt light and comfortable in his hand, like it was meant to be there. Jack had pulled the blade from solid rock, in the basement beneath the school, then used the weapon to defeat Zarnik, one of General Gore's warriors. Chancellor Rex, headmaster of Hero Academy, had told Jack that the sword once belonged to the General himself.

Jack pointed the blade at the spider and crept towards it. "Almost ..." he muttered. But when he was just one step away, the robot scuttled straight up the cliff, out of sight.

Danny ran his hands through his floppy dark hair. "You've got to be joking!"

Ruby was already climbing up the sheer cliff-face. "What are you two waiting for?" she yelled down. "Do you want Olly's team to catch their spider first?"

This time Jack and Danny both groaned. If Olly and his team won, they'd never hear the end of it.

"We're coming!" they yelled together.

Despite Jack's super-strength, the climb wasn't easy. The cliff was slippery and his feet kept sliding off the footholds. Seagulls shrieked and swooped around them. As they climbed higher, Jack could see the island's rugged coast curving towards a black fortress, half hidden by clouds — Hero Academy.

"Can you see the spider yet?" he called up to Ruby. She shook her head.

Beside Jack, Danny went still. He pushed back his hair, revealing large ears that were pointed like a bat's.

"I can hear it," Danny said. "There!" He pointed up at a ledge of rock jutting from the cliff. The spider was clinging to it.

Around the spider's ledge, the cliff-
face was as smooth as glass. There
were no handholds.

"How are we going to get it?" Ruby
wondered aloud.

"Trust your powers," said a voice
next to them.

Jack looked around, startled, to see a fourth figure clinging to the cliff — a dark-skinned woman with bright purple hair. It was Ms Steel, one of their teachers. She could teleport and had a habit of turning up when she was least expected.

"Er, hello, Ms Steel," said Jack.

"Trust your powers," Ms Steel said again, with a mysterious smile. "Remember."

Then she vanished.

Jack blinked. "What did she mean?"

Danny frowned thoughtfully, looking up at the spider again. "I think I know," he said slowly. "Ruby, can you blast the ledge?"

Ruby grinned. "No problem."

Her orange eyes began to glow. With
a sizzle, streams of burning flames
shot from them, slicing right through
the ledge of rock. It plummeted down,
taking the spider with it.

Jack shot out his hand as it fell
past. His golden fingers closed around
the spider, plucking it from the rock,
which smashed on to the beach
below. "Got it!"

Danny whooped. "Good catch!"

The robot powered down, curling
itself into a tight ball. Jack stowed
it safely in his backpack, and they

began climbing down the way they'd come.

"I just hope we've beaten Olly," said Ruby. "He'll be so—"

"Shhh," interrupted Danny suddenly. "Something's coming. I can hear it."

He was looking out to sea. Jack followed his gaze. On the horizon glittered the skyscrapers of Ventura City — Jack's home. Then Jack spotted something hurtling towards them. It was the size of an eagle, but as it flew closer, Jack realised it wasn't an ordinary bird at all. Its bat-like wings beat furiously and its long, cruel beak was open wide. Strapped to the creature's back was a strange metal tube.

"What is it?" he breathed.

A bolt of blue light shot from the metal tube, sizzling towards them.

*Boom!*

The ball of light struck the cliff-face with a blast so loud, it seemed to have exploded inside Jack's head. A shower of bright sparks almost blinded him.

"We're under attack!" Jack yelled, ears ringing. "Let's go!"

Check out Book Two:
ATTACK OF THE BAT ARMY
to find out what happens next!

# WIN AN ADVENTURE PARTY AT GO APE TREE TOP JUNIOR*

## WITH

**TEAM HERO**

## How would you like to win an epic party at Go Ape! for you and five of your friends?

You'll get up to an hour of climbing, canopy exploring, trail blazing and obstacles and a certificate to take away too!

The Go Ape! leafy hangouts are the perfect place to get together for loads of fun and prove that you've got what it takes to be the ultimate hero.

For your chance to win, just go to

## TEAMHEROBOOKS.CO.UK

and tell us the names of the evil creatures that feature in the four different Team Hero books.

## Closing date 31st October 2017

PLEASE SEE the website above for full terms and conditions.
*SUITABLE FOR 4 - 12 years old, but open to any age child over 1m tall.

IN EVERY BOOK OF TEAM HERO SERIES ONE there is a special Power Token. Collect all four tokens to get an exclusive Team Hero Club pack. The pack contains everything you and your friends need to form your very own Team Hero Club.

# FREE TEAM HERO CLUB PACK

## MEMBERSHIP CARDS · MEMBERSHIP CERTIFICATE · STICKERS · POWER GAME · BOOKMARKS

Just fill in the form below, send it in with your four tokens and we'll send you your Team Hero Club Pack.

SEND TO: Team Hero Club Pack Offer, Hachette Children's Books, Marketing Department, Carmelite House, 50 Victoria Embankment, London, EC4Y 0DZ.

CLOSING DATE: 31st December 2017

## WWW.TEAMHEROBOOKS.CO.UK

✂ - - - - - - - - - - - - - - - - - - - - - - - - - - - -

ease complete using capital letters *(UK and Republic of Ireland residents only)*

RST NAME

URNAME

ATE OF BIRTH

DDRESS LINE 1

DDRESS LINE 2

DDRESS LINE 3

OSTCODE

ARENT OR GUARDIAN'S EMAIL

I'd like to receive Team Hero email newsletters and information about other great Hachette Children's Group offers (I can unsubscribe at any time)

*Terms and conditions apply. For full terms and conditions please go to teamherobooks.co.uk/terms*

*TEAM HERO Club packs available while stocks last. Terms and conditions apply.*

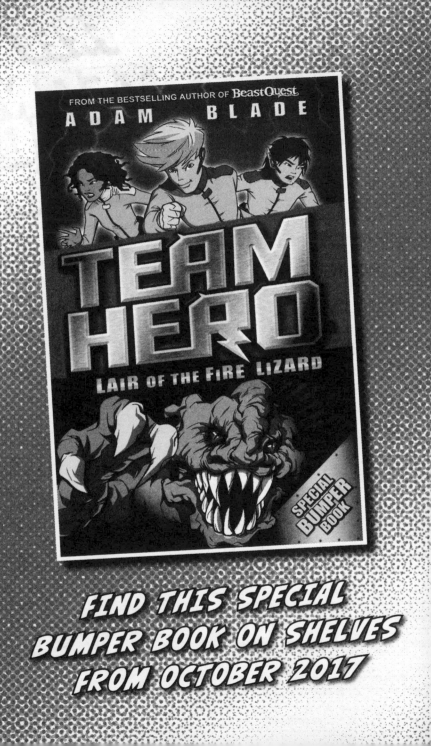

FROM THE BESTSELLING AUTHOR OF BeastQuest

# ADAM BLADE

# TEAM HERO

## LAIR OF THE FIRE LIZARD

SPECIAL BUMPER BOOK

FIND THIS SPECIAL BUMPER BOOK ON SHELVES FROM OCTOBER 2017

# Go Ape!
## TREE TOP JUNIOR

# BIRTHDAY PARTIES

at 18 locations UK wide

**PARTY BAGS** 🌲 **PARTY ROOMS** 🌲 **T-SHIRTS**

# Find out more at goape.co.uk
## or call 0845 094 8813†